For Margot.
—MM

For my family, my friends,
and Eunice.
—DD

Text copyright © 2001 by Miriam Moss
Illustrations copyright © 2001 by Delphine Durand

First published in Great Britain in 2001
by Orchard Books London
Miriam Moss and Delphine Durand assert
the right to be identified as the author
and the illustrator of this work.

Library of Congress Cataloging-in-Publication Data available.
ISBN 0-439-36835-9

10 9 8 7 6 5 4 3 2 1   02 03 04 05

Printed in Singapore   46

First Edition, August 2002

Scritch Scratch

written by
Miriam Moss

pictures by
Delphine Durand

Orchard Books • New York
An Imprint of Scholastic Inc.

One day
a tiny insect,
no bigger than a freckle,
crawled into Ms. Calypso's classroom.

Nobody noticed. . . .

Ms. Calypso went on calling the roll.
Ruby undid Polly's braid.
Joshua painted on Peter's back.
And Sammy trimmed Mark's bangs.

crops

mops

drops

tops

2 + 2
=

5
351
741

The little louse had no wings.
But she had six strong legs,
and she climbed straight into the Spelling Ship
hanging above Ms. Calypso's head.

What a wonderful view!
Miss Calypso's cascading curls
and the students' short hair, long hair,
parted hair, braids, pigtails, ponytails...
even a frizzy wig on the plastic skeleton in the corner!

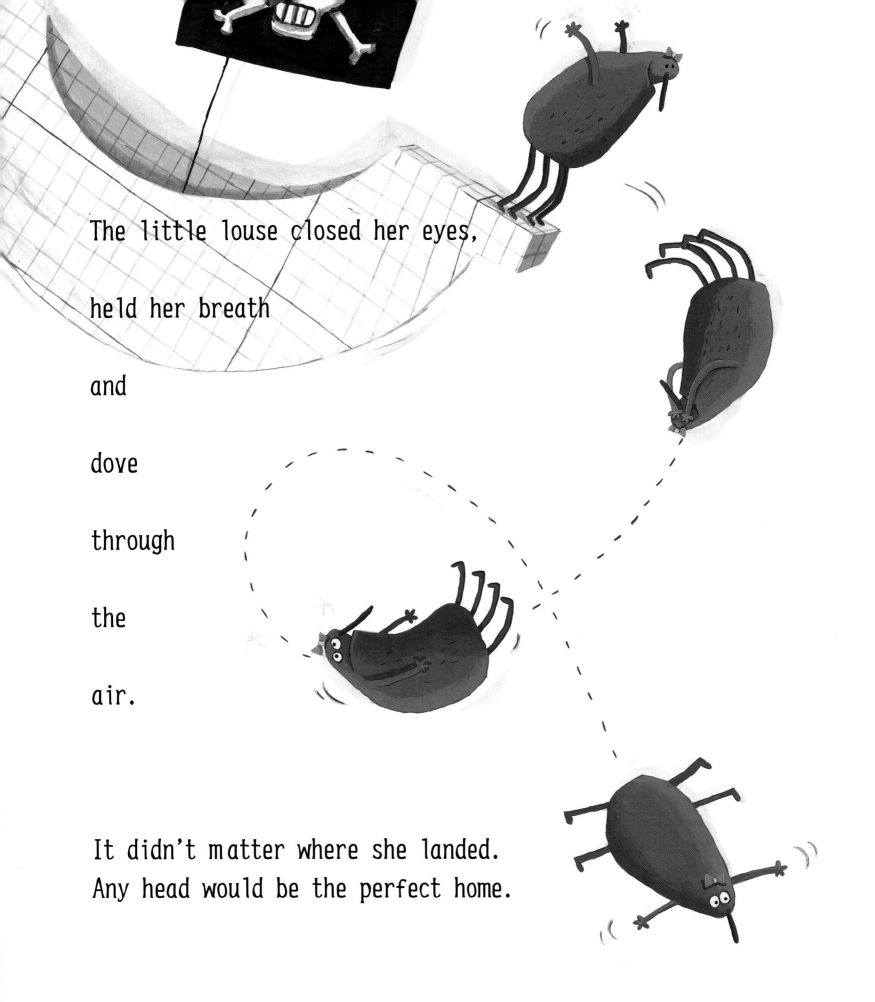

The little louse closed her eyes,

held her breath

and

dove

through

the

air.

It didn't matter where she landed.
Any head would be the perfect home.

And the perfect home she landed on was...

Ms. Calypso!
The little louse got to work right away,
sticking one tiny egg to each
hair on Ms. Calypso's head.

She sang a happy tune.

Oh... No one knows from where I came,
A nit, a nibbler with no name,
But watch the teacher scritch and scratch,
When my creepy, crawly babies hatch.

Before long, the creepy, crawly babies did hatch.
And they climbed into Ms. Calypso's cascading curls.

Scritch Scratch went Ms. Calypso,
            praising Polly's pirate picture.

Scamper Scamper went the tiny head lice,
            dancing down Polly's braid.

From

then on,

whenever

two

heads

touched,

lots of

little

head lice

moved

home!

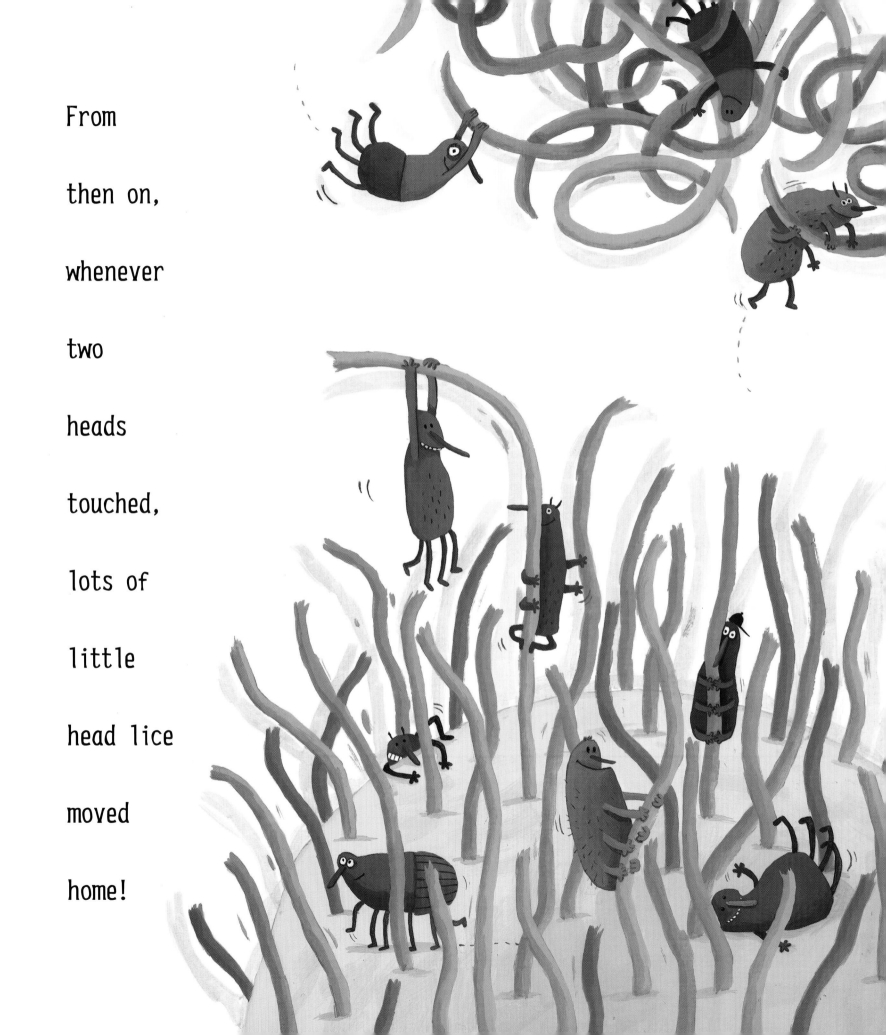

Scritch Scratch went Polly,
playing with Ruby's hair.

Scamper Scamper went the head lice.

Scritch Scratch went Joshua,
drawing on Peter's back.

Scamper Scamper went the head lice.

Scritch Scratch went Sammy
trimming Mark's bangs.

Scamper Scamper went the head lice.

In no time at all,
the little lice had perfect homes
of their very own. . . .

And that was when Mr. Trout, the principal, strode in.
"May I speak with you, Ms. Calypso?" he asked.
Ms. Calypso agreed to meet him at lunchtime
to discuss the scratching problem.

That night Mr. Trout sent letters home
to all the parents.

Dear Parents,
Please comb special conditioner
through your children's hair
and make it so slippery
that all the head lice
slide into the bath water
and float away.

The next day the conditioned and combed
children returned to school.
There was not a single louse in sight.
They were all gone.

Well,
all
except
one!

The little louse was still on Ms. Calypso.
You see, Ms. Calypso lived alone.
She had no one to help condition and comb her hair.

Oh...

(sang the little louse, who was now a grandmother)

No one knows from where we came,
We nits, we nibblers with no name,
Watch the children scritch and scratch,
When more creepy, crawly babies hatch.

Scritch Scratch went Ms. Calypso.

Scamper Scamper went the head lice.

And soon the whole class was
scritching and scratching all over again!

Mr. Trout sent another note home.
He went to see Ms. Calypso.
And there, in a little room, Mr. Trout found
himself offering to wash Ms. Calypso's
hair for her.

That night, while Mr. Trout conditioned and combed Ms. Calypso's hair, they fell in love. He fell in love with her cascading curls, and she fell in love with his mustache.

So Mr. Trout and Ms. Calypso got married.
And now if you look into Mrs. Trout's classroom—
what do you see?

Mrs. Trout still calls the roll.
Ruby still undoes Polly's braid.
Joshua still paints on Peter's back.
And Sammy still trims Mark's bangs.

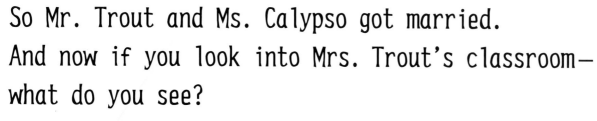